Stop, Look, and Listen

Written by Alison Hawes

We stop,
we look,
and we listen for cars
before we cross the street.

We stop,
we look,
and we listen for trucks
before we cross the street.

We stop,
we look,
and we listen for motorcycles
before we cross the street.

We stop,
we look,
and we listen for buses
before we cross the street.

We stop,
we look,
and we listen for traffic...

and then we cross the street.